All Aboard TRUCKS

A Platt & Munk **ALL ABOARD BOOK™**

 Published simultaneously in Canada. Printed in the U.S.A. Library of Congress Catalog Card Number: 87-72333 ISBN 0-448-19094-X
B C D E F G H I J

The illustrations in this book have previously appeared in *The Big Book of Real Trucks*, published by Grosset & Dunlap.

On front cover: gooseneck trailer

SCISSORS TRUCK

All Aboard TRUCKS

By Lynn Conrad
Illustrated by Richard Courtney

SNOW PLOW

Platt & Munk, Publishers

Trucks in the Neighborhood

All kinds of trucks do jobs around the neighborhood. A sanitation truck picks up garbage and hauls it away. The workers throw the garbage into a large compartment called the hopper. Then a big blade crushes the garbage and pushes it to the back. All of the trash is squeezed together tightly to make room for more.

SANITATION TRUCK

A street cleaner is fun to watch! It sprays water on the street and has big brushes that sweep up the dirt along the curb. This street cleaner has two steering wheels. The driver can clean either side of the street without changing the truck's direction.

STREET CLEANER

MOVING VAN

A family is moving away to a new house. Workmen load the furniture into a long moving van. Inside, there are padded mats that protect the furniture from nicks and scratches. Everything is strapped down to stay in place while the van travels. All the furniture in the house fits neatly inside this one big truck!

A fuel truck makes an oil delivery to a neighbor's house. The oil is pumped through a hose from the truck right into the storage tank in the basement. Now the house will be warm and cozy inside when it is cold and nasty outside.

FUEL TRUCK

DUMP TRUCK

A dump truck fills a hole around a newly laid drainpipe. The truck has a dump box in the back that holds a load of dirt, sand, and rock. The driver uses special controls to lift the box. Then the load tumbles out on top of the new pipe.

The mechanical arm on a cherry picker lifts a worker high enough to reach telephone wires that need repair.

Trucks Around Town

Different trucks work hard all around the town. A tow truck tows away cars that have broken down or have been in an accident. A bread truck delivers fresh bread and cakes and pies from the baking company to the stores where the baked goods will be sold. A mail truck delivers letters and packages from the post office to people's homes and businesses.

TOW TRUCK

BREAD TRUCK

MAIL TRUCK

Ginnie's Mart
FRESH
MILK
Deli Sandwiches 99¢
T&R

A beverage truck delivers juice, soda, and other drinks sold in bottles and cans to a grocery store. Inside the truck are compartments that hold the beverage cases tightly and keep the bottles from bouncing and breaking when the truck moves. Each compartment has its own door so the driver can easily get to the cases he needs.

BEVERAGE TRUCK

218-801
BZ-1197

Some trucks are so big and strong that they can carry other trucks and cars! This car transport is delivering new pickup trucks to a dealer. The trucks are fastened to the trailer so they won't fall off. The trailer has movable ramps. When the driver makes a delivery, he raises or lowers the ramps and drives each truck right off the trailer and onto the dealer's truck lot.

CAR TRANSPORT

The tanker trailer delivers gasoline to a gas station. The tanker holds different grades, or types, of gasoline in separate compartments. To unload the gasoline, the driver attaches hoses to valves at the bottom of the tanker. Then the fuel is pumped into underground storage tanks at the station.

TANKER TRAILER

PUMPER

Pumper and ladder trucks fight fires together. The pumper carries hoses and has a special pump that can send out hundreds of gallons of water every minute. The ladder truck carries rescue equipment, first-aid kits, and long ladders that can reach up to high floors in tall buildings.

LADDER TRUCK

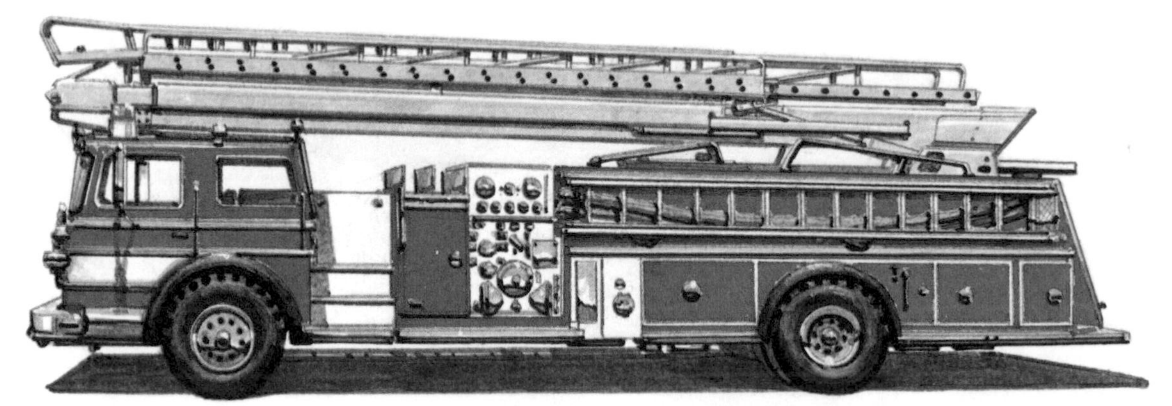

BOOKMOBILE

The bookmobile goes all over town to bring books to people who live far away from the library. Inside this small truck are shelves that can hold nearly 2,000 books! The vendor truck is a snack bar on wheels. The driver can stop at a factory or a park and sell hot dogs, drinks, and ice cream. If there are no hungry people in one place, the vendor can drive to another lively spot.

VENDOR TRUCK

Trucks in the Country

Trucks are on the move in the country. Big tractor trailers go all over, transporting all kinds of freight. The cab where the driver sits is the tractor. The long box at the back is the trailer. A refrigeration unit is attached to this trailer to keep food cool or frozen. Sometimes this type of trailer is called a reefer.

TRACTOR TRAILER

LOG-STACKER

In the forest a log-stacker loads a pole trailer. Its big forked clamp carries several logs at a time. The pole trailer has U-shaped beams to hold the logs in place. After the logs are stacked, they are fastened with strong chains to keep them from sliding off when the truck travels to the lumber mill.

POLE TRAILER

At a road construction site, a concrete truck mixes sand, cement, gravel, and water together. The mixer turns constantly to keep the concrete moist. When the concrete is just right, it is poured down a chute into waiting molds that will form the highway.

CONCRETE TRUCK

The off-road dump truck is one of the biggest trucks around. The huge wheels on this gigantic truck are taller than the driver. They are strong enough to carry tons and tons of earth and rock over rough ground.

OFF-ROAD DUMP TRUCK

Livestock trucks carry animals to livestock markets. Cattle, chickens, pigs, or sheep travel in pens inside the trailer. It has openings to let in fresh air. This trailer has different levels so small animals, like chickens, can travel on the top level and larger animals, like pigs, can travel down below.

LIVESTOCK TRUCK

A motor home is really a traveling house. Inside there is space for living quarters, a bath, and a kitchen—all with built-in furniture. People who have motor homes can travel long distances and always have a place to spend the night.

Look around. Everywhere you turn, trucks are on the go!

MOTOR HOME